This Walker book belongs to

....

....

....

To Lydia,
S.M^c^B.

For the mice,
Julian and Mami,
A.J.

First published 2007 by Walker Books Ltd
87 Vauxhall Walk, London SE11 5HJ

This edition published 2015

10 9 8 7 6 5 4 3 2 1

This book has been typeset in Cochin.

Printed and bound in China.

British Library Cataloguing in Publication Data: a catalogue record for this book is available from the British Library.

ISBN 978-1-4063-5970-1

www.walker.co.uk

GUESS HOW MUCH I LOVE YOU *in the* AUTUMN

Written by
Sam McBratney

Illustrated by
Anita Jeram

WALKER BOOKS
AND SUBSIDIARIES
LONDON • BOSTON • SYDNEY • AUCKLAND

Little Nutbrown Hare
and Big Nutbrown Hare went out
in the autumn wind.

On a windy day
the leaves are blowing.

They chased after falling leaves
until Big Nutbrown Hare
could chase no more.

“I have to have a rest!” he said.

Then a big brown box came rolling
by, blown by the autumn wind.
Little Nutbrown Hare caught
up with the box when it got
stuck in a bush.

What a fine big box!
It was great for
jumping over …

jumping on …

and jumping in.

Big Nutbrown Hare was resting
under a tree when a box
appeared in front of him.
A big brown box.
It gave one hop and then
stood absolutely still.

"I'm a box monster!"
shouted the box.

Goodness me!
Big Nutbrown Hare
blinked his eyes and
wondered if he was
dreaming, for he had
never heard of a box
monster before.

The box, or the monster –
or maybe the box monster –
took two hops forward.

“Here I come!” roared the box,
hopping its biggest hop yet,
and Big Nutbrown Hare
jumped behind the tree.

"I wonder should I run
away!" said Big
Nutbrown Hare.

"No!" shouted the box, which suddenly flew into the air. "It's only me!"

And there was Little Nutbrown Hare, who could hardly stop laughing.

"You're not a monster,"

said Big Nutbrown Hare.

"But guess what."

"What?"

"I'm a big nutbrown monster –

and I'm coming to

get you!"

And so he did.

Other *Guess How Much I Love You* Books

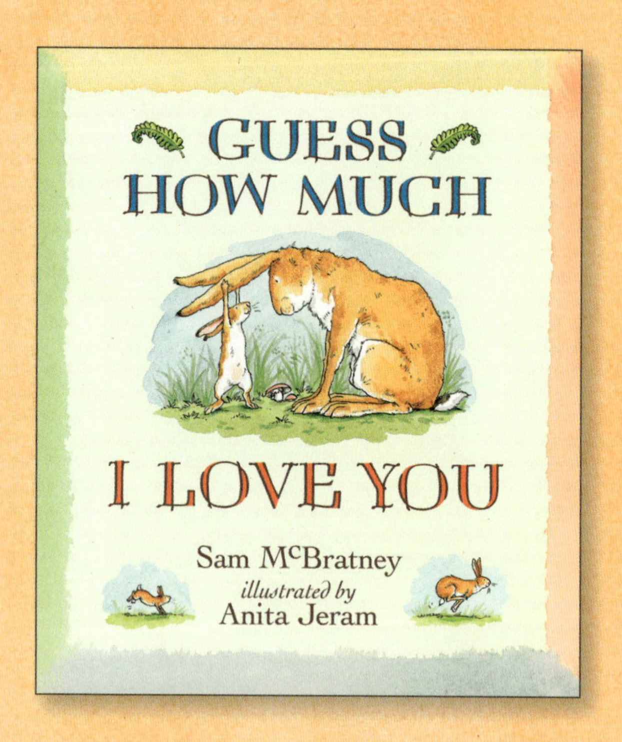

With more than 28 million copies sold, *Guess How Much I Love You* is one of the world's best-loved picture books.

The endearing simplicity of Sam McBratney's story and Anita Jeram's exquisite watercolours make it a modern classic.

ISBN 978-1-4063-0040-6

Available now

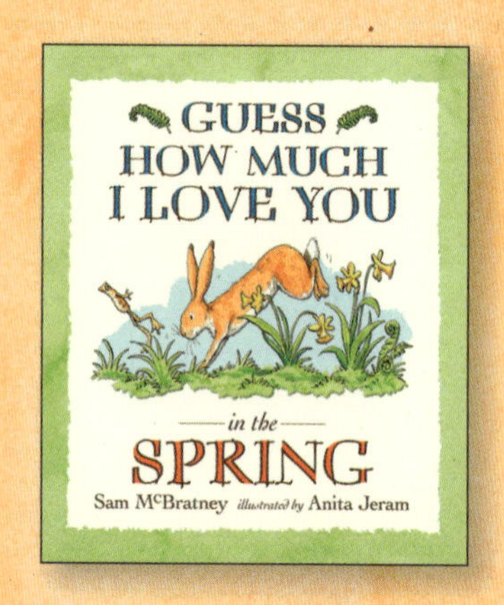

ISBN 978-1-4063-5743-1

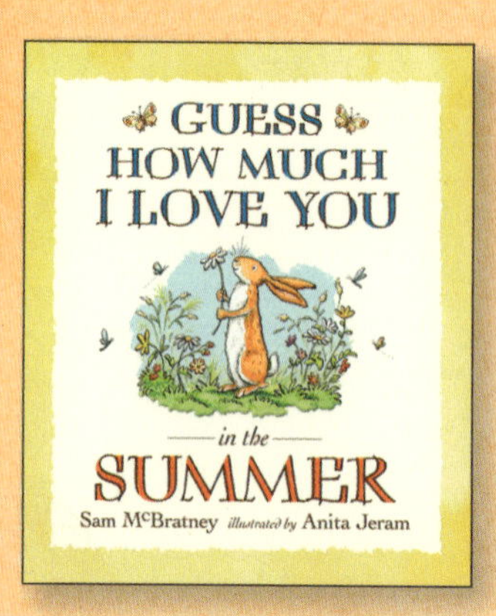

ISBN 978-1-4063-5817-9

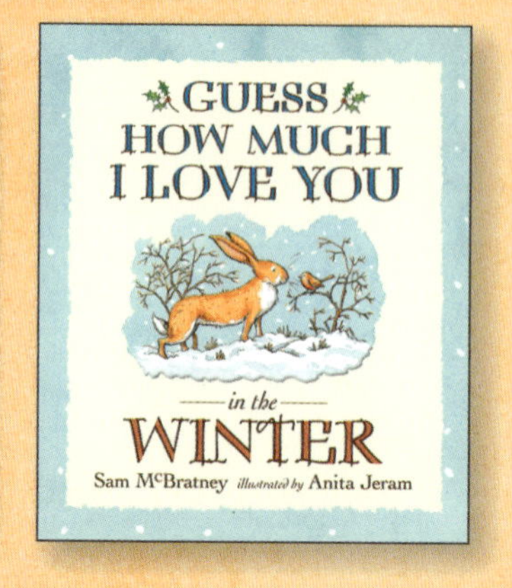

ISBN 978-1-4063-5428-7

Coming soon to all good booksellers

www.walker.co.uk